W9-BSM-364

# Even Higher

RICHARD UNGAR

———

*Adapted from a story by I.L. Peretz*

Tundra Books

Published in Canada by Tundra Books,
75 Sherbourne Street, Toronto, Ontario M5A 2P9

Published in the United States by Tundra Books of Northern New York,
P.O. Box 1030, Plattsburgh, New York 12901

Library of Congress Control Number: 2006909046

LIBRARY AND ARCHIVES CANADA CATALOGUING IN PUBLICATION

Ungar, Richard
Even higher / Richard Ungar.

Adapted from: If not higher.
ISBN 978-0-88776-758-6

1. Jews – Folklore.  2. Rabbis – Folklore.  I. Peretz, Isaac Leib,
1851 or 2-1915  If not higher.  II. Title.

PS8591.N42E94 2007          j398.2089'924          C2006-905773-7

We acknowledge the financial support of the Government of Canada through the Book
Publishing Industry Development Program (BPIDP) and that of the Government of
Ontario through the Ontario Media Development Corporation's Ontario Book Initiative.
We further acknowledge the support of the Canada Council for the Arts and the Ontario
Arts Council for our publishing program.

ONTARIO ARTS COUNCIL
CONSEIL DES ARTS DE L'ONTARIO

*Medium: watercolor and colored pencil on paper*

PRINTED IN HONG KONG, CHINA

1 2 3 4 5 6          12 11 10 09 08 07

In memory of Grandpa Isidore,
also known as "Never Stuck"

Reuven couldn't believe his ears. "Yossel," he said, "you want me to spy on our own rabbi?"

"Don't think of it as spying," answered Yossel, picking up a stone and skipping it, "think of it as solving a mystery."

"Yes, a great mystery," said Menachem, letting fly his own stone.

"What mystery are you talking about?" asked Reuven.

"Haven't you heard?" said Yossel, bending down to pick up another stone. "Each year, on the day before Rosh Hashanah, our rabbi is nowhere to be seen. It is as if he vanishes into thin air. At night he comes back, but no one sees where he goes during the day." Yossel flung the stone and it skipped twice before disappearing. "Do you know what everyone is saying, Reuven? That our beloved rabbi ascends to heaven and spends the day there, pleading with the Master of the Universe to forgive the sins of the people of Nemirov."

Reuven laughed. "And you believe that, Yossel? Come now. Surely our rabbi cannot fly like a bird."

"Maybe; maybe not," replied Yossel. "But tomorrow is the day before Rosh Hashanah, and it is your job to find out for sure!"

"Yes, Reuven, it is your job," echoed Menachem.

"My job? Why me?" asked Reuven.

"It is simple," said Yossel. "Of the three of us, you are the smallest and the quickest, and you have good eyesight. This job requires great speed, the ability to hide in tight spaces, and sharp eyes."

Reuven was about to protest, but then his curiosity took hold. "All right," he said, as they turned and headed back to the village of Nemirov. "I will find out once and for all where our rabbi goes on the day before Rosh Hashanah."

That evening, Reuven stood outside the synagogue and pressed his nose to the glass. Sure enough, there was the familiar sight of the rabbi greeting the congregants. Just then, the rabbi sneezed and took half a step backwards. Reuven smiled. *How could a man who was almost blown over by the force of his own sneeze have the power to ascend to heaven?* He pushed the window open a crack and listened as the rabbi addressed the small group.

"One kind of giving to the poor," began the rabbi, "is to give after you have been asked. A higher kind is to give before you have been asked. And an even higher kind of giving is when the identity of the giver is not known to the person receiving the gift."

With a last look through the window, Reuven hurried to the rabbi's empty house, slipped inside, and hid.

It was not long before the rabbi arrived home, washed, and lay down to sleep. Reuven held his breath and stayed as still as he could.

After a few moments, the rabbi's breathing became even. *He's asleep,* Reuven thought, allowing himself to relax slightly. *I'll just rest for a few moments.*

Reuven was awakened by the chirping of birds. A ray of sunlight pierced the gloom. *Oh, no!* he thought. *It's morning. What if the rabbi has already gone out?*

Reuven was about to crawl out from under the bed, when he heard a thump. A bony ankle appeared inches from his nose. He breathed a sigh of relief. *The rabbi has not gone yet!* He waited until he heard the front door close. Then he scrambled from his hiding place and ran to the window.

At first, he didn't see the rabbi. In fact, there was no one in sight except a woodcutter. But the next moment, the woodcutter sneezed and took half a step backwards. Reuven almost cried out. *It's the rabbi, in disguise!*

Reuven slipped out of the rabbi's house and followed, keeping a
safe distance behind.

*He's heading for the synagogue,* thought Reuven. *Of course!* He couldn't
wait to tell Yossel and Menachem that he had solved the great
mystery of where the rabbi goes on the day before Rosh Hashanah.

But to Reuven's astonishment, the rabbi didn't stop at the
synagogue. He kept on walking.

*Hmm,* thought Reuven. *If he isn't going to the synagogue, then he must surely be going to the cheder. What devotion to learning!*

But to Reuven's surprise, the rabbi didn't stop at the cheder either.

Reuven's mind raced. *Where could the rabbi possibly be going?* They were approaching the outskirts of Nemirov. Only a handful of houses remained. Reuven could see the line of trees marking the edge of the great forest in the distance.

He sniffed. The aroma of freshly baked bread filled his nostrils. *Aha,* thought Reuven, wondering why he had not thought of it before. *The rabbi must be going to Beryl the Baker's house!* Everyone knew that the rabbi was very fond of Beryl's bagels. *And the reason for his woodcutter disguise must be to bargain for a better price,* Reuven figured.

Reuven was so sure he was right that he began to turn around. But just then, out of the corner of his eye, he saw the rabbi walk right past Beryl's house. Completely baffled, Reuven followed as the rabbi left the village and entered the great forest.

After a while, the rabbi stopped at a clearing, where some newly cut trees lay on the forest floor. Reuven hid and watched as the rabbi pushed up his shirtsleeves and hoisted an ax high over his head.

Reuven couldn't believe his eyes. *The rabbi of Nemirov chopping wood?*

From his hiding place, Reuven saw the rabbi's woodpile grow larger and larger. Morning passed into afternoon and still the rabbi hacked away, pausing only to drink some water from a flask.

Reuven began to wonder if he would have to spend the whole day there, when the rabbi finally laid down his ax and grabbed a bundle of the chopped logs.

Treading carefully, so as not to make any noise, Reuven followed the rabbi along a path that snaked deeper into the forest. *Where is the rabbi going?*

Reuven thought hard. Then he remembered that this path led to the house of Mottel the Tailor and his wife, Shayna. *But didn't Mottel pass away last year?*

Soon Mottel's modest house came into view. From his perch high up in the gnarled branches of an oak tree, Reuven watched as the rabbi knocked lightly on the door.

After a moment, Reuven heard a woman's frail voice: "Who is there?"

"It is I," the rabbi answered, "a woodcutter from the village. With firewood to sell."

"Thank you," said the feeble voice, "but I have no money for firewood."

Reuven watched in amazement as the rabbi opened the door and walked in.

Reuven counted to ten and then snuck into the cold house, hiding himself inside a narrow closet. He hugged his arms to keep warm.

Peeking out, Reuven saw Shayna, Mottel the Tailor's widow, huddled beneath the blankets of her bed, shivering.

"It is very dark in here," said the rabbi. "Perhaps you do have some money, but it is just too dark to find it. With your permission, I will light a fire in the fireplace. Then, by the light of the fire, perhaps we can find some money by which I can be paid."

Reuven saw Shayna give a weak nod to the rabbi, who carried his bundle of stout logs over to the fireplace.

Before long, the tiny house filled with warmth and light. Above the crackle of the logs, Reuven heard the rabbi say to Shayna: "I am afraid you are right. I have looked everywhere, and you do not have any money to pay me. But who knows what the future holds? After all, is it not a favorite saying of your rabbi that the Holy One will provide? Let us make a bargain. When the Holy One provides you with money, you will pay me. And, just so that you will not miss seeing the money when it arrives, I will keep this fire lit for you." With that, the rabbi heaped more logs on the fire.

Reuven watched as the old woman nodded. Her cheeks appeared to have a bit more color. The rabbi turned to leave and, just in time, Reuven ducked back behind the closet door. He waited until Shayna fell asleep, then tiptoed out of the house.

No sooner had Reuven arrived back in Nemirov than Yossel and Menachem came running up to him.

"Reuven, did you see where he goes?" asked Yossel, breathlessly.

"I did," replied Reuven.

"Well?" said Menachem. "Don't keep us waiting! Is it true? Did the rabbi ascend to heaven?"

For a moment, Reuven was silent. Then he looked at his friends, nodded, and said softly, "Even higher."